All Together Now

For Danny

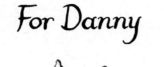

ISBN 0-439-18785-0

Copyright © 1999 by Anita Jeram.
All rights reserved.
Published by Scholastic Inc., 555 Broadway, New York, NY 10012,
by arrangement with Candlewick Press.
SCHOLASTIC and associated logos are trademarks and/or registered
trademarks of Scholastic Inc.

12 11 10 9 8 7 6 5 4 3 2 1   0 1 2 3 4 5/0

Printed in the U.S.A.   08

First Scholastic printing, September 2000

This book was typeset in Kabel Book Alt and hand-lettered.
The illustrations were done in watercolor and ink.

All Together Now

Anita Jeram

SCHOLASTIC INC.

New York Toronto London Auckland Sydney
Mexico City New Delhi Hong Kong

When Mommy Rabbit says,
"All together now,"
one thing Bunny, Little Duckling,
and Miss Mouse often do is sing
their special little Honeys song.

"All together now!" . . .

We're the little Honeys.
A little Honey is sweet.
Quack quack, squeak squeak,
Thump your great big feet!

In the little Honeys song,

"A little Honey is sweet" is Bunny's special line.

Bunny was Mommy Rabbit's first little honey,

before Little Duckling and Miss Mouse came along.

He was always as sweet as can be.

That's why Mommy Rabbit called him

"Bunny, my Honey."

In the little Honeys song, "Quack quack"

is Little Duckling's special line.

Its special meaning is,

I'm yellow and fluffy and

good at splashing and sploshing.

It means, even if I don't look like a bunny,

Mommy Rabbit's still my mommy just the same.

When he was born,

Little Duckling came from an egg.

The first surprise was when he hatched.

Bunny was just peeping at the egg

when it cracked open and out

came Little Duckling.

The next surprise was when
Little Duckling followed Bunny home
and became his brother and
the second little Honey.

In the little Honeys song, "Squeak squeak"

is Miss Mouse's special line.

Its special meaning is,

I've got a pink itchy-twitchy nose

and a pink squirly-whirly tail.

It means, even if I don't look like a bunny,

Mommy Rabbit's still my mommy just the same.

Miss Mouse first arrived when Bunny

and Little Duckling found her all alone in the

long grass early one summer morning.

Miss Mouse wasn't frightened.

She just seemed to need some

love and affection.

Mommy Rabbit soon made

her one of the family,

a new sister and a third little Honey.

As well as singing their special song,
the little Honeys play all sorts
of special games together.

They play splashy-sploshy games,

which Little Duckling

is best at.

They play itchy-twitchy,

squirly-whirly games,

which Miss Mouse

is best at.

They play run-rabbit-run games,

which Bunny is best at.

Best of all, they play the

Thump-Your-Great-Big-Feet game,

which they are all best at together

because they all have

Great Big Feet.

Bunny has

Great Big Feet.

Little Duckling has
Great **Big** Feet.

Miss Mouse has
Great **Big** Feet.

And sometimes
Mommy Rabbit
plays with them,

which is extra-specially special

because Mommy Rabbit has the

Greatest,

Biggest

Feet of all!

The Thump-Your-Great-Big-Feet game goes like this:

thump!

thump!

thump!

thump!

thump!

We're the little Honeys.
A little Honey is sweet.
Quack quack, squeak squeak,
Thump Your Great Big Feet!